Magnus

NECRON 3

catalan communications
new york

Also Available
by
Magnus

NECRON
NECRON 2

NECRON 3
ISBN 0-87416-107-X

Written and Illustrated
by Magnus

Translated by
Philip Haworth

Edited by Bernd Metz

Published by Catalan Communications
43 East 19th Street
New York, NY 10003

First Catalan Communications Edition
July 1991

10 9 8 7 6 5 4 3 2 1

Dep. L.B. 15.438/91
Printed in Catalonia (Spain)

OFF THE COAST OF NORWAY...
WE'LL RETURN HERE WHEN WE CAN MAKE FULL USE OF THE MINES LEFT TO US BY THE LATE GENERAL KOMMEL.
MISTRESS! LOOK!
SHIT! THE FUEL GAUGE IS DROPPING!
DAMN!
A STORM! THAT'S ALL WE NEED!
LET'S HOPE OUR LITTLE BIRD CAN STAND IT.

BWAMP
CARRIED BY THE TURBULENCE, THE SEAPLANE LOSES COURSE...
... AND VEERS SOUTHWEST.
I'VE LOST CONTROL AND I CAN'T MAKE A SEA LANDING – THE WAVES WILL SWAMP US!
THERE! WE'RE AS LOW AS WE CAN GET!
NECRON AFRAID, MISTRESS!
DON'T BOTHER ME! NOT NOW!
IF THIS CONTINUES, WE'RE DOOMED!
UHHHH!
LUCK, HOWEVER, BRINGS A CURRENT OF WARM AIR...
WE'RE OUT OF THE CENTER OF THE STORM!

BUT NOW IT'S TOO LATE TO GET BACK TO THE NORTHEAST COAST!...WE'LL HAVE TO MAKE A STOP OFF IN NORMANDY.
..RRRRUMBL!
NORMANDY GOOD! NECRON EAT NORMANDY.
CRETIN! NORMANDY'S A FRENCH PROVINCE.
FLYING OVER THE SEINE...
DOWN THERE'S A COVE THAT'S ISOLATED ENOUGH TO LAND IN WITHOUT ATTRACTING ANY ATTENTION.
JUST IN TIME. THERE ISN'T A DROP MORE GAS.
TAKE ME TO LAND, WE'LL TRY AND FILL UP SOMEWHERE.
URG!
QUICK, HIDE THE DINGHY!

LET'S MAKE A QUICK TOUR.
NECRON HUNGRY!
CHOMP CHOMP CHOMP.
AS THE SUN RISES...
SWISC
KRUMP
NECRON EAT...
SLÚP
HI HIHI'' HI'''
WHAT THERE?
A HORSE! QUICK, HIDE IN THE BUSHES!
...HORSIE?!? SHE WOMAN WITH FOUR LEGS?
NO! IT'S A HORSEWOMAN ON A HORSE. THERE'S TWO OF THEM!
HORSIE? GOOD TO EAT?
SILENCE! THEY'RE COMING!
GALOP GALOP GALOP
GALOP GALOP

COUNTESS GERALDINE FRONTENAC, THE OWNER OF BARRÉ FOREST, IS AN EARLY RISER...
WHOAH, MISTRAL!
SHE'S LEFT HER HORSE AND IS HEADING FOR THAT CABIN. PERFECT! I'M GOING TO FIND OUT ABOUT SOME GAS!
HORSIE!
IF ANYONE SEES YOU, IT'LL SCREW EVERYTHING UP!
NECRON GO WITH MISTRESS?
FORGET IT!
YOU MUST STAY HIDDEN, UNDERSTAND?
IT STILL HASN'T SUNK INTO HIS DENSE HEAD THAT HE'S DIFFERENT FROM EVERYONE ELSE.
SNIFF...
NECRON TOO UGLY!
MISTRESS ASHAMED OF NECRON!
ME SO UNHAPPY!
ME VERY HUNGRY!
HiHiHiiiii
HORSIE!

HIHIHIHIH
YUM!
STRASC
SMAK
STOP IT, HORSIE!
NECRON EAT... SNORT... BUT NECRON SAD TO BE SO UGLY... CHOMP...
GNAM GNAFF GNAF
SHE'S GONE INSIDE!
I HAVE TO GET GAS, BY HOOK OR BY CROOK!
TRAK
?
OH, JULIAN, SUCH TIGHT JEANS...DON'T THEY CRAMP YOUR STYLE?
HA! HA! HA!
...WELL, AS THE GAMEKEEPER, I HAVE TO KEEP THE BIRDS HAPPY!

...AND THIS IS MY PERSONAL HUNTING GROUND!
I HOPE I'M NOT DISTURBING YOU?
OH! BARONESS WUNDER, I PRESUME. PLEASE EXCUSE ME... I JUST HAVE SOMETHING TO TAKE CARE OF.
UGH! A LIVING MAN'S MEMBER!
TAKE YOUR TIME, PLEASE!
SHE'S MISTAKEN ME FOR SOMEONE ELSE... I'LL PLAY ALONG WITH IT AND SEE WHAT HAPPENS!
UHH! UHH!
SLUP
UMM! MMHH!
CIOMP CIOMP
OH! AAHH! OOOH! OHH!
POMP POMP POMP GLU GLU
ALWAYS...BURP ...SO PLENTIFUL, JULIAN!
BULP

A GOOD CIGAR AND A BLOW JOB... THE ONLY WAY TO START THE DAY...
DON'T PAY ANY ATTENTION TO JULIAN, HE'S A JOKER! I ALWAYS COME HERE FOR BREAKFAST.
I SEE... I SEE...
ACTUALLY, EVEN THOUGH WE DON'T KNOW EACH OTHER PERSONALLY, I WAS SURE YOU WOULD ACCEPT MY INVITATION.
OH, YES?
...AND THEN I WAS SO DISAPPOINTED WHEN YOU CHANGED YOUR MIND. WE ARE SO CURIOUS TO MEET YOU!
OH WELL... I CHANGED MY MIND AGAIN.
MAGNIFICENT! YOU CAME IN YOUR PLANE?
CORRECT!
THIS IS AN EXCEPTIONAL OPPORTUNITY. POSING AS BARONESS WUNDER, I HAVE TO GET THE MOST OUT OF THIS SITUATION.
BUT I CAN'T FIND MY MISTRAL ANYWHERE... HE WAS TIED UP THERE... NEARBY.
JULIAN! JULIAN!
HEY, COUNTESS! LOOK AT THIS!

OHHH! POOR MISTRAL! MUST BE THE WOLVES...
...THE WOLVES?!?
OH, IT'S AWFUL! I'LL HAVE TO RETURN TO THE CHATEAU IN JULIAN'S TRUCK! ARE YOU COMING, BARONESS?
UHM, NO... I WILL COME FOR DINNER...
I HAVE A LITTLE SOMETHING TO SEE TO!
NECRON!
ANOTHER OF YOUR SCREW-UPS! YOU'LL STAY HUNGRY FOR THREE DAYS FOR THAT!
SWAP SWAP SWAP SWAP
OW! OW! OW!
NOW, COME ON. YOU NEED A HIDING PLACE!
NECRON NOT HIDE! NO!
OH YES YOU WILL. I'M THE GUEST OF COUNTESS FRONTENAC.
...SIGH! MISTRESS ASHAMED OF NECRON.
LOOK, NECRON, A CEMETERY!
IT'S SO NICELY KEPT... ANYWAY...
PAX

TAKE THIS SHOVEL!
AND DIG HERE!
THERE'S THE COFFIN! TAKE IT OUT.
UH!
TUNK
OPEN IT UP!
WE WON'T BE NEEDING THAT!
SFRASC
NOW GET INSIDE!
GULP!
NECRON NOT GET IN COFFIN, NO!
OHH NOOO?
AT DUSK, A HEARSE MAKES ITS WAY TOWARD CHATEAU FRONTENAC...
THIS UNDERTAKER'S CARRIAGE IS A STROKE OF GENIUS! THE HOSTS WILL TAKE ME FOR A SOME SCREWBALL ARISTOCRAT WITH SLIGHTLY MACABRE TASTES.
CLOP CLOP
CLOP CLOP

GRRR!
CLOP CLOP CLOP
... AS FAR AS THE REAL BARONESS IS CONCERNED, SHE SAID SHE WASN'T COMING. I HOPE SHE DOESN'T CHANGE HER MIND!
CLOP CLOP CLOP
GOD! WHAT A JOINT! MUST BE WORTH MILLIONS!
CLOP CLOP
CLOP CLOP
MY DEAR... WHAT A DELICIOUS IDEA, YOUR CAR.
F
YOU DON'T MIND IF I'M FAMILIAR?
YOU CAN PARK TO THE RIGHT OF THE STABLES...
...AND THE COFFIN? WHAT'S IT FOR?
JUST A PERSONAL THING... I TAKE IT EVERYWHERE!
THEY'LL TAKE IT UP TO YOUR ROOM. COME ALONG, I'LL INTRODUCE YOU.

THIS IS PRINCESS FRANZISKA VON WALDSTEIN...
COUNTESS MADDALENA LANZI DI SAN SEVERO...
...DUCHESS ISABELLE RODRIGO VARGAS DE ARAGON.
...AND THIS, MY DEARS, IS BARONESS WUNDER, MY NEW FRIEND!
TO THE HEALTH OF THE ARISTOCRACY!
NOBLESSE OBLIGE!
YOU'RE JUST IN TIME...I HAVE A HABIT OF RULING ON CERTAIN CASES OF UNRULINESS AMONG THE SERVANTS. IT'S DIVERTING SPORT WHICH GIVES US AN APPETITE, BEFORE SITTING FOR DINNER.
BRING IN THE FIRST CASE!
HERE HE IS! JAKE, THE GARDENER!
I'M SORRY! I'M SO ASHAMED! MERCY, PLEASE!...

SCIAK
SCIAK
SHUT UP, MINION!
OW! OWW! OW!
HE WAS OGLING BRIGITTE IN THE BATH AND WAS JERKING OFF.
I'M A LONELY MAN... TRY TO UNDERSTAND!
AH! VOYEUR! DON'T YOU FIND YOUR DEVIANT BEHAVIOR DISGUSTING?
...THE PRESS.
WICKED HUNCHBACK! WE'LL IRON YOUR BACK OUT FOR YOU.
DIRTY, SLEAZY COCKROACH!
NO! NO!
I WASN'T JERKING OFF.
...I JUST TOUCHED MYSELF A LITTLE...
...A TINY, LITTLE BIT...
HELP!
HELP!
ON WITH THE PUNISHMENT!
TLANG
TIK TIK TIK TIK
TIK
SKRUMPSC
BLUURGH! HOW HORRIBLE! BLOOD AND GUTS EVERYWHERE... QUICKLY, CLEAN UP, BRIGITTE.
YES, MADAME.

SNAP
BRING ON THE SECOND ONE!
WHAT? JULIAN?
COUNTESS!... WHAT'S HAPPENING? I DON'T UNDERSTAND...
THE GAMEKEEPER JULIAN HAS BEEN BOASTING AROUND THE TOWN MARKET THAT HE HAS HAD ORAL CONTACT WITH HER LADYSHIP AND CALLING HIMSELF "THE SPERM BANK OF CHATEAU FRONTENAC!"
BUT IT WAS JUST A JOKE!
HOW AWFUL! THAT DESERVES PUNISHMENT! ...
I PROPOSE THE "IRON MAIDEN" OR THE "MALAYAN TONGS"...
WE COULD MAKE HIM DRINK UNTIL HE BURSTS... ALL WE NEED IS A FUNNEL, A SINK AND A TUBE TO PUT DOWN HIS THROAT...
YOU ARE FAMOUS FOR YOUR REFINED SADO-MASOCHISM, MY DEAR... WHAT DO YOU SUGGEST?
HMM... LET'S SEE... ONE IDEA GIVES RISE TO ANOTHER.
WE COULD BEGIN BY CUTTING HIS FLESH...
CUT OFF HIS BALLS? NOT BAD!

NO! IT'S VERY SIMPLE... A FEW NICKS IN THE RIGHT PLACES...
THE HONOR IS ALL YOURS...
...AFTERWARD, I WANT TO TRY FOR MYSELF.
AH!!!! AH!!!
ZIK
ZIK
ZIK
ZIK
AND NOW WE SPRINKLE HIM WITH SOME CRYSTALS OF NaCl!
AMAZING! BUT WHAT IS IT?
SODIUM CHLORIDE, OR MORE SIMPLY... TABLE SALT!
AHI AHI
AHIIIUUH
SALT HIM! SALT HIM!
I WANT TO SALT HIM AS WELL!
WHAT A LOVELY TORTURE!
OH!
OH!
OH!
OH, BAD LUCK! NO MORE SALT!
SO, SHALL WE COOK HIM?
SUPERB! LET'S GET A SPIT!

...HE LOOKS DONE TO ME!
...HMM...PERHAPS A TOUCH OF ROSEMARY, OR SOME WHITE WINE!
BUT, NO! WE'RE NOT CANNIBALS!
HA! HA! HA!
SHALL WE EAT NOW?
MEANWHILE, ON AN UPPER FLOOR OF THE CHATEAU...
HEY... WHAT COULD BE IN THIS COFFIN?
IT'S TOO HEAVY TO CONTAIN JUST CLOTHES! WHAT IF IT'S DYNAMITE?
WANT A LAUGH? LET'S HAVE A LOOK!
AHHHH!
A MONSTER!
NECRON NOT MONSTER!
KLING
GRRR
IT SPEAKS!
LUCKY HE'S CHAINED. HE CAN'T HURT US!
KLING

AFTER ALL, HE'S GOT A NICE FACE!
KLING
WHAT ABOUT THAT PIECE OF WEAPONRY BETWEEN HIS LEGS? WHAT DO YOU SAY? THINK HE'LL PLEASE OUR LITTLE COUNTESS?
ABSOLUTELY! I'LL CALL HER STRAIGHT AWAY!
HMM, REALLY?
EXCUSE ME, I MUST DISAPPEAR FOR A MINUTE!
ON SEEING NECRON!
BUT... HE'S MAGNIFICENT!
ME?
WHAT A WHOPPER!
...ENORMOUS, HUH?
I'VE NEVER SEEN THE LIKE!
I MUST TRY IT!
SLURP SLURP
UMGRRR!

AAAHHH! HOW WONDERFUL!
I WANT HIM... FOR ME AND ME ALONE!
I'M GOING TO PAMPER HIM, CARESS HIM, THIS BIG BRUTE...
MY MISTRESS BAD TO NECRON...
...THIS MISTRESS BETTER!
I WILL GIVE HIM THE BEST FOOD...
I'LL TREAT HIM WELL, LIKE POOR MISTRAL!
SLURP...
UNBIND HIM AND TAKE HIM TO MY ROOM... I'LL CONVINCE BARONESS WUNDER THAT HE'S ESCAPED...
AS YOU WISH COUNTESS!
AFTER DINNER...
BARONESS WUNDER!
BARONESS WUNDER?!
SHIT!

COUNTESS, PLEASE FORGIVE THIS SUDDEN ARRIVAL...
IN FACT, AFTER YOU RECEIVED MY MESSAGE, I CHANGED MY MIND...
AND HERE I AM!
I'V ALREADY HEARD THAT SOMEWHERE ELSE... YOU! WHO ARE YOU?
I AM FRIEDA BOHER!
I'M SO EMBARASSED!
AND I CONSIDER MYSELF THE MOST BRILLIANT MIND IN THE WORLD! AS FOR YOU...
YOU'RE ALL IN MY POWER.
HANDS IN THE AIR!
OH!
I SAID, HANDS IN THE AIR!
BANG
TLUK
SCHEMING WITCH!
WLAM
EH?
TLUMP
BITCH! SHE KILLED BRIGITTE!
FRANCINE. TAKE AWAY POOR BRIGITTE... TOMORROW WE'LL PUT THE INCINERATOR TO WORK... FOR NOW, LET THE PARTY CONTINUE!

DAMN IT!
I WAS RIGHT OVER THE TRAP DOOR.
I'VE HURT MYSELF!
COMPLIMENTS OF THE COUNTESS!
DESSERTS! DRINKS!
FRUITS!
PASTRIES!
BLUURGH!
SPLIT
SPLAT
YOU DON'T LIKE SUGAR? TRY THIS CAVIAR!
KONG
NOT GOOD!
WHAT COULD HIS FAVORITE DISH BE?
TELL US WHAT YOU LIKE, DEAR.

HORSIE!
LIVING HORSIE!
GULP!
HOR...SIE?
HOW IS MY BIG HUNK?
AHEM...
HE WANTS TO EAT A LIVE HORSE!
WHAT SHALL WE DO? HE'LL HAVE TO GO DOWN TO THE STABLES.
NOW I UNDERSTAND!
IT'S YOU WHO ATE MY POOR MISTRAL! BAD BOY!
DON'T YOU LIKE ANYTHING ELSE?
YES. MISTRESS' PUSSY!
PUT THAT IN HERE!
NECRON LIKE HEADS AND TAILS!

AT THE SAME TIME...
GERALDINE! GER...
DEAREST GERALDINE! YOU TOLD US THE PARTY WOULD BE WOMEN ONLY!
HEY, GIRLS! GERALDINE'S FOUND A SUPER-STUD AND SHE'S PUTTING OUT FOR HIM!
A SUPER-STUD, HERE!
AND SHE'S KEEPING HIM FOR HERSELF!
MMM!
C'MON GIRLS! LET'S ORGY!
HURRY UP, GERALDINE! I'M AFTER YOU!
OHH... ZUBLIME!
AH AH AH
HUM!

THOSE BITCHES ARE BOUND TO HAVE FOUND NECRON... I CAN ONLY RELY ON MYSELF TO GET OUT OF HERE...
THESE OLD PLACES ARE FULL OF FORGOTTEN DUNGEONS AND...
GOT YOU! DO YOU THINK YOU CAN SCARE ME?
GAK
...AND SECRET PASSAGES!
SKRRUNNG
ALL RIGHT! I HIT THE RIGHT SPOT. THERE'S THE PASSAGE!
GERALDINE AND HER CRONIES ARE GOING TO PAY FOR THIS!
AND I SHALL SAVOR THE MOMENT!
FROM VAULT TO VAULT...
...SHE REACHES THE ARMORY...
THIS SWORD WILL DO THE JOB!
SGUISC

I CAN HEAR THEM GIGGLING.
FILTHY BITCHES!... ERK!
NECRÓN!
YOU DIRTY, NO-GOOD SCUZZ!..
LET GO OF THOSE WOMEN IMMEDIATELY!
EVEN BETTER... I ORDER YOU TO TIE THEM UP.
OBEY! OR ELSE I'LL CASTRATE YOU WITH THIS SWORD!
DON'T LISTEN, DARLING. IF YOU WANT TO STAY WITH US, I'LL BE YOUR MISTRESS!
UHM.
UHM... NEW MISTRESS KIND!
...IF YOU BETRAY ME... I WILL MAKE YOU PAY DEARLY!
BUT OLD MISTRESS NASTY!
WELL?
YES, MISTRESS!

DIRTY BEAST!
AHHH!
ACH!
HEEELP!
WELL DONE! NOW BIND THEM WELL!
NOW LET'S SEE, WHERE'S THE MEDICINE CABINET?
NOT BAD! SLEEPING PILLS AND TRANQUILLIZERS...
SECONIL
Nembutal
benzopam
LIBRUM
QUIETIN
SPEED AND ANTI-DERESSANTS!
RITAVIL
I'LL GRIND UP A GOOD DOSE AND...
FSSSSCCH
AN IMPROVISED SYSTEM, BUT THE SOLUTION IS READY...
OWN!
DOES IT HURT? NEVER MIND... NEARLY DONE!
THIS BIG SAFE INTERESTS ME...
STORK

GOOD LORD! THERE'S A FORTUNE HERE!
Cartier Paris
HOW GHASTLY! WHAT HAVE YOU DONE TO US?
I FEEL WEIRD ALL OVER!
I'VE SIMPLY TESTED ONE OF MY BRILLIANT INVENTIONS ON YOU. NOW, WITH YOUR PERMISSION, I'M LEAVING. COME ON, NECRON.
I'LL HAVE TO ABANDON MY LOVELY PLANE... THANKS TO JULIAN'S TRUCK WE CAN GAIN SOME TIME!
AS FOR YOU, WE'LL DEAL WITH YOU LATER, YOU PIG!
SOB!
PARIS, GARE DU NORD...
A SLEEPER TO AMSTERDAM, PLEASE.
YOU'RE PUTTING THAT IN THE CABIN?!
OUTTA THE WAY!
SHIT... SO HEAVY. WHAT'S INSIDE... GOLD BARS?
ENOUGH HUMOR, CREEP. NOW GET LOST.

I WONDER IF MY POTION HAS HAD ANY EFFECT YET?
DAMN...
GOD...DAMN...
I...I'M...CHO...
...CHO... CHOKING!
MY HAIR! MY BEAUTIFUL HAIR!
AAAGGHHH!
OF COURSE, IT'S HARD TO GROW OLD SO QUICKLY...
WELL, WHILE THE TRAIN IS GOING, I'LL CATCH UP ON A LITTLE FASHION...
VOGUE
BUT, SOMEONE, YOU'LL FIND OUT WHO, HAS ESCAPED FRIEDA'S TERRIBLE MIXTURE, AND...
WE'LL MEET AGAIN!

ON A TRAIN BOUND FOR AMSTERDAM, FRIEDA BOHER, NECRON'S PERFIDIOUS MISTRESS CAN'T RESIST ADMIRING HER BOOTY...
MMHH! THIS'LL FETCH A GOOD PRICE IN AMSTERDAM...
AT THE VERY LEAST, MILLIONS OF DOLLARS WHICH WILL ALLOW HER TO PURSUE HER INFAMOUS DREAMS OF POWER AND DOMINATION.
THERE IT IS, IT'S JUST A QUESTION OF BEING ALERT...
AND IN A FEW HOURS, I'LL HAVE ENOUGH CASH TO MINE THE URANIUM DEPOSITS! *
ELLE
* SEE NECRON 2
TUM
TUM
TUM
WHAT IS IT, STUPID MONSTER?
LLE
NECRON OUT, MISTRESS... NECRON WANT FUCK!
NO!
ELLE
YOU SHOULDN'T HAVE DISOBEYED ME. YOU'RE PUNISHED! I WILL NOT ALLOW YOU TO TOUCH ME.
ELLE
GULP!

IF NECRON NOT FUCK MISTRESS, MISTRESS NOT FUCK ANYMORE...
!
HOLD ON! YOU'VE GIVEN ME AN IDEA!
I'M GOING TO MAKE YOU DIE OF DESIRE!
CLIK
GET OUT!
UH, YES!
YOUR BACKWARD BRAIN HAS SHOWN ME HOW TO MAKE YOU SUFFER THE MOST!
LICK!
SLURP!
OH!
LAP
LAP
LAP
THIS FUCKING CORPSE REALLY HITS THE SPOT!

OHH... YES... YEEESS...
NOW THAT'S ENOUGH!
STONK
NO!
MORE! MORE!
I SAID, NO!
NECRON CAN'T STOP. NECRON WANT MORE!
HA! HA! H! I ONLY EXCITED YOU TO MAKE YOU SUFFER MORE. NOW DO YOU UNDERSTAND?
URG!
AND IF THAT MAKES YOU SQUIRM, YOU DESERVE IT, CRETIN!
THE EXPRESS SPEEDS THROUGH THE NIGHT...
613
SNCF
MAY I SIT HERE? THERE'S NO MORE ROOM!
OF COURSE, BE MY GUEST, MADAM!
IN THE DINING CAR.

THESE OVERNGHT JOURNEYS ARE HIDEOUSLY BORING... I SUFFER FROM INSOMNIA AND THERE'S ONLY ONE CURE FOR IT.
OH, YES... AND WHAT'S THAT?
I'D LIKE TO TELL YOU ABOUT IT... IN PRIVATE!
?
IN YOUR CABIN PERHAPS?
...ANOTHER HOT ONE!
I THINK YOU GET IT!
NUMBER 15. I'LL BE WAITING!
AT MIDNIGHT?
AT MIDNIGHT!
TILL LATER!
AND THAT'S WORK... MMH... NICE ASS...
FLIC
restaurant
...TO STEAL THE SECRET DOCUMENTS THAT HE'S TAKING TO BRUSSELS!
BAH! THESE EUROPEAN POLITICIANS ARE ALL FOOLS!
GOODNIGHT, MADAME!
THAT IDIOT BIT FIRST TIME. IF HE KNEW I WAS BEING PAID BY HIS POLITICAL ENEMIES...

KLUK
URG...
GRRRMMF...
FZZZT
FZZ
FZIT
LOCK NOT CLICK.
GNIK
MISTRESS SLEEPING.
MISTRESS NOT HEAR NECRON GET OUT...
NECRON CLEVER.
IF THEM SEE NECRON, THEM SHOUT!
NO PEOPLE. NECRON NOT SEEN. NOT CAUGHT.
5
NECRON WANT TO FUCK!

OH NO, NO! I DON'T LIKE IT LIKE THAT...
?
THERE! LIKE THAT! GOOD!
...IT FITS LIKE A GLOVE!
YES! YES!
THAT'S IT! YES! BRAVO!
TUNF TUNF TUNF
YOU STOP!
SKRAK!
NECRON WANT WOMAN!
EH?
AHH!
PATABUMP TUMP
SILENCE!
...MMGLE! ...RGLE!
OH! YOU BRUTE!
HUH?
OH! RAM IT UP ME!
ZUMP

GLARP!
OH! OH! OH!
ZUM ZUM ZUM
HUH?
ZUM!
...
UH?
AARGH!
YOU NOT WOMAN! YOU DIRTY OLD MAN!
NECRON LEAVE!
AAAHHH!
CRAK
SFLASC
AHH! WHAT HAVE YOU DONE, YOU WRETCH!
YOU'VE TORN ME AP... ART...
TUNF
HIM DEAD!

NECRON SLIP OUT.
OK. I'LL GO AND SEE IF EVERYTHING'S IN PLACE!
PEOPLE?
ME GO IN HERE!
NECRON INVISI-BLE!
?
HERE ALREADY? COME IN! HAVE A DRINK!
I'M ALMOST READY...
...FOR YOU...
AAAHHH!
YEESS?
OH!

WOMAN WAITNG FOR NECRON. REAL WOMAN!
EVEN BETTER THAN MISTREES FRIEDA!
...HMM...
MISTRESS FRIEDA!?!
IF MISTRESS WAKE UP AND NOT FIND NECRON! SHE WILL BEAT! NECRON RETURN NOW!
OH!
AHHH!
SHH!
CRAK
SHHH!

HMM - WHAT TIME IS IT?
CLIK
SHIT! SON-OF-A-BITCH! HE'S ESCAPED AGAIN!
I HAVE TO FIND HIM IMMEDIATELY...
... BEFORE ACCIDENTS START HAPPENING!
TUMP TUMP
OH, SORRY!
TUMP
WHAT A RUSH! I BET THAT HIS TYPE IS MEETING WITH SOME LITTLE WHORE!
AHEM!
KNOK NOK
IT'S ME, MISS.
NO REPLY! BUT THE DOOR IS AJAR!
MMHH!
ARE YOU ALREADY ASLEEP?
TUMP

GULP!
SLAM
DEAD!... SHE'S DEAD!
PARDON ME SIR, BUT IS THIS YOUR CABIN?
WHAT? I... ERR... NO! THAT IS TO SAY...
TUMP
I HAD A RENDEZVOUS... AND... LOOK FOR YOURSELF!
IN GOD'S NA... YOU KILLED HER!
SNCF
WHAT ARE YOU SAYING... I DON'T KNOW ANY MORE THAN YOU. WHEN I ARRIVED, SHE WAS ALREADY DEAD!
OH YES! HEY, JACK! KEEP AN EYE ON HIM!
YOU GOT IT!
SNCF
SNCF
A CRIME ON MY TRAIN! WE'LL HAVE TO STOP AT THE NEXT STATION AND ALERT THE POLICE!
WHA...? WHAT'S ALL THIS HULLABALLOO?
TRAK TRAK TRAK
NOTHING, NOTHING! A WOMAN'S BEEN KILLED.
MY GOD! HOW TERRIBLE! WHO DID IT?
A DIPLOMAT?... AND HE STRANGLED HER?

STRANGLED?!?
THAT'S ONE OF NECRON'S FAVORITE METHODS. I HAVE TO FIND HIM OR WE'RE BOTH IN FOR IT!
WHAT THE HELL!?
HEEELPP!
CRASK
WHAT NOW?
THERE... IN THERE! ALL DEAD!... THEY GOT THE ENGLISH COLONEL!
SNCF
O LORD! IT'S SICK! THE COLONEL!... AND HIS NEPHEW!
SNCF
YARENNE STATION... I'LL ALERT THE TRANSPORT POLICE IMMEDIATELY.
VARENNE
BUT WHY'VE YOU STOPPED?... CAN'T YOU SEE THE GREEN LIGHT?
613
CHIEF'S ORDERS! THERE'S BEEN A CRIME!
TERRIFIED BY ALL THE COMMOTION...
NECRON AFRAID. NECRON HIDE.
WC
STRONG

WHA...?!
SKRANG
AGHH!
HHHEEEEELLPPP!
THEY ALL SCREAM WHEN SEE NECRON!
OUCH!
NECRON NOT MONSTER!
THE STATION-MASTER HAS STOPPED THE TRAIN! THREE MURDERS!
YES...AND THEY'VE GOT A SUSPECT!
LET'S HURRY! THE 748 IS ARRIVING IN THIRTY MINUTES.
HAVE YOU CALLED FOR REINFORCE-MENTS?
YES, THEY'RE ON THEIR WAY.
LET'S GO! LET'S GO!
THIS CHARACTER WAS CAUGHT AS HE WAS SNEAKING OUT OF THE CABIN OF THE MURDERED WOMAN.
BUT I'D ONLY JUST ARRIVED!
SNCF
I OPENED THE DOOR AND SAW HER LIKE THAT... SPREAD-EAGLED!
DID YOU KNOW THE VICTIM'S NAME?

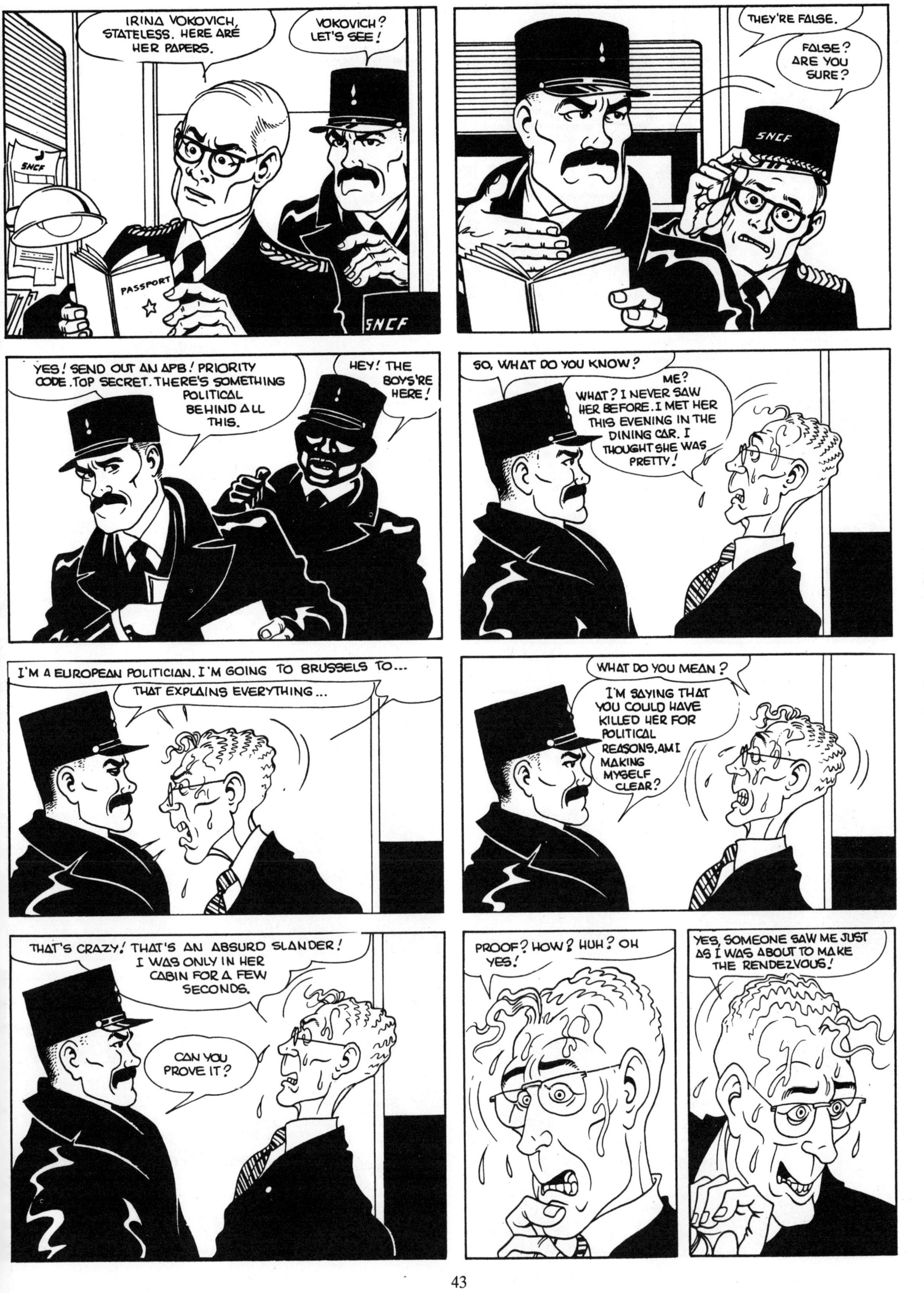
IRINA VOKOVICH, STATELESS. HERE ARE HER PAPERS.
VOKOVICH? LET'S SEE!
SNCF
PASSPORT
SNCF
THEY'RE FALSE.
FALSE? ARE YOU SURE?
SNCF
YES! SEND OUT AN APB! PRIORITY CODE. TOP SECRET. THERE'S SOMETHING POLITICAL BEHIND ALL THIS.
HEY! THE BOYS'RE HERE!
SO, WHAT DO YOU KNOW?
ME? WHAT? I NEVER SAW HER BEFORE. I MET HER THIS EVENING IN THE DINING CAR. I THOUGHT SHE WAS PRETTY!
I'M A EUROPEAN POLITICIAN. I'M GOING TO BRUSSELS TO...
THAT EXPLAINS EVERYTHING...
WHAT DO YOU MEAN?
I'M SAYING THAT YOU COULD HAVE KILLED HER FOR POLITICAL REASONS. AM I MAKING MYSELF CLEAR?
THAT'S CRAZY! THAT'S AN ABSURD SLANDER! I WAS ONLY IN HER CABIN FOR A FEW SECONDS.
CAN YOU PROVE IT?
PROOF? HOW? HUH? OH YES!
YES, SOMEONE SAW ME JUST AS I WAS ABOUT TO MAKE THE RENDEZVOUS!

THAT WOMAN!
I'M SURE THAT SHE NOTICED ME AS WE PASSED IN THE CORRIDOR.
WELL, MADAM?
CERTAINLY, I REMEMBER IT WELL.
...YOU SEE! I'M CLEAN.
COULD YOU SAY HOW LONG HE WAS INSIDE THE CABIN?
LET'S SEE NOW...YES! I'D SAY ABOUT TWENTY MINUTES.
THAT'S A LIE! SHE'S LYING!
WHY WOULD I LIE?
GOT YOU! YOU'RE UNDER ARREST!
THIS IS AN ERROR OF JUDGE-MENT!
CLAK
NOW, WHILE THEY'RE BUSY WITH THAT IMBECILE, THEY'LL STOP SEARCHING THE TRAIN. PERHAPS THAT POLITICO-CREEP WILL EVEN BE CHARGED WITH HOMOSEXUALITY!
ARE WE LEAVING YET?
WHAT A SCAN-DAL!
2
THERE'S THE COMMISSIONER. WE CAN TAKE OFF THE BODIES NOW.

IT'S SWARMING WITH COPS! I HOPE NECRON'S KEEPING HIS HEAD DOWN.
BRING THAT TO ME.
OH... I FEEL SICK!
UMPH
RUTT
WC
UMPH
HEY! YOU CAN'T USE THE BATHROOM WHILE THE TRAIN IS STANDING.
SNCF
AAARGH!
WHAT ARE YOU DOING? USE THE SINK!
GLUURGH. BARF. GARGLE.
PLOP
PLOP
IN THE SINK...
THERE'S BEEN ANOTHER MURDER.
BUT HOW...?
THEN THE KILLER IS STILL AMONG US?
NO ONE CAN GET OFF.
HE'LL GET US ALL.
SEARCH THE CARS, ONE BY ONE!
...PANIC SWEEPS THE TRAIN...

DAMNATION! THAT MONSTER IS EVEN MORE SAVAGE THAN I THOUGHT!
...SO, HE DESERVES TO BE LEFT TO HIS FATE...
DUPONT! HAS THE FREIGHT ALREADY BEEN SEARCHED?
WELL, FROM WHAT I KNOW... I THINK IT MIGHT HAVE, CAPTAIN TRUDEAU... MAYBE... I MEAN, I'M NOT SURE...
EXPRESS
31
BUT, HE'S MY MASTERPIECE! I CAN'T LEAVE HIM! WHERE CAN HE BE HIDING?
WHAT D'YOU WANT?
POLICE! WE'RE REQUISITIONING THIS TRAIN, THERE'S A KILLER ON BOARD.
IN HERE? NO WAY! I HAVEN'T MOVED EXCEPT TO TAKE A PISS AND GRAB A COFFEE. THERE'S NO KILLER HERE!
WE'LL SEE. DUPONT, CHECK THESE CASES!
IT DOESN'T SEEM WISE TO GO IN THERE, CAPTAIN.
YOU'RE A COWARD, DUPONT. FRANCE WASN'T BUILT BY COWARDS!
3171
37
WAIT UNTIL I BECOME A COMMISSIONER. I'LL GIVE YOU A MEDAL, DEAR CAPTAIN!
QUIET, WIMP!
IF YOU WANT TO RISK YOUR NECK, THAT'S YOUR BUSINESS!
FRAGILE

I HEARD HIM! ...HE'S IN HERE!
FRAGILE
URG!
IS HE THERE?
CRANK
BANG
I'M WOUNDED!!
HELP ME, DUPONT!
UUUGHH! A NAKED MAN!
14
PLUMP
JUST ONE MINUTE, YOU BASTARD!...
A MONSTER!
URG!
KONG
KONG
KONG
TAKE THAT! AND THAT!
HELP ME!
CLAK
ESCAPED BY A HAIR!
SKRRRAAANNG

HEELP! IT'S A WILD, NAKED MADMAN. I'VE MANAGED TO LOCK HIM IN HERE!
HE'S GOT A HUGE TOOL! AND LOOKS LIKE A CORPSE! MUST BE A SATYR!
A SATYR!
PANT
WHY NOT?! ALL THESE CRIMES HAVE A SEXUAL FOUNDATION!
YEAH! AND HE'S TEARING UP THE FOUNDATIONS NOW!
SBONG
SKONG
SKRANG
GRRRGROARR
ZOW
ZOW
ZOW
ZOW
GET THE PASSENGERS INTO THEIR CABINS, WE'LL COVER THE WAGON DOORS.
DON'T SHOOT IF THERE'S A RISK OF HITTING A PASSENGER!
AHH! AHHH!
GRRRR!
AHHHH!

FUCK! I HAVE TO DO SOMETHING!
...LIKE STARTING THIS DAMN TRAIN!
WHERE'RE YOU GOING, MADAME?
TO MY COMPARTMENT. THEY SAY THERE'S A MONSTER LOOSE ON THE TRAIN.
THAT'S RIGHT, MADAME. BUT DON'T YOU WORRY, IF I SEE HIM, I'M GOING TO BLOW HIS HEAD OFF WITH THIS BABY!
OF COURSE YOU ARE!
AND NOW...
RIGHT, CHILDREN... START HER UP... WE'RE OFF!
DID YOU HEAR? START THE FUCKING TRAIN!
...START THE TRAIN? BUT WHO ARE YOU?
DON'T BE A WISEGUY OR YOU'LL TASTE THIS! NOW, GO!
YES, YES! WE'RE GOING!

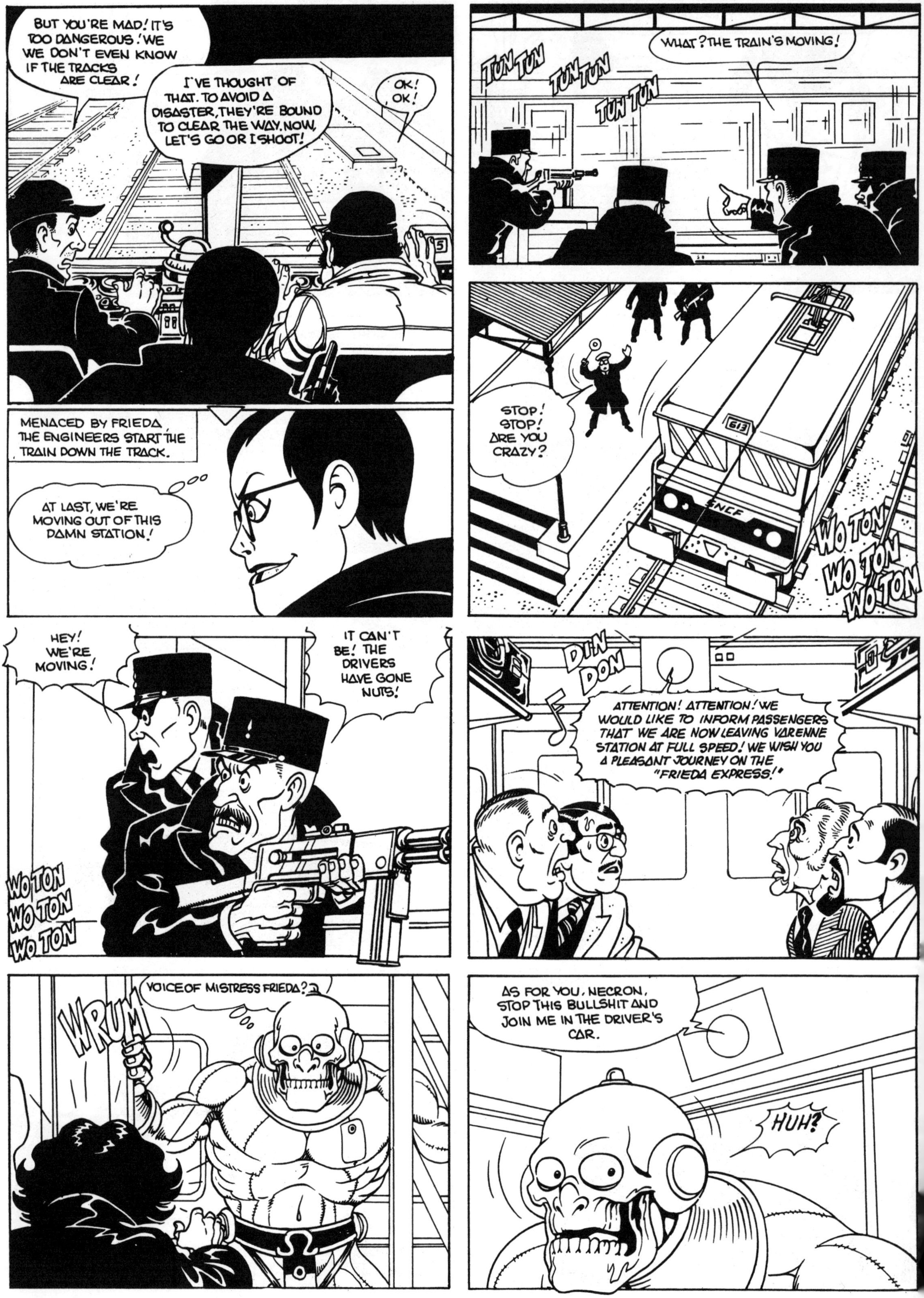
BUT YOU'RE MAD! IT'S TOO DANGEROUS! WE WE DON'T EVEN KNOW IF THE TRACKS ARE CLEAR!
I'VE THOUGHT OF THAT. TO AVOID A DISASTER, THEY'RE BOUND TO CLEAR THE WAY. NOW, LET'S GO OR I SHOOT!
OK! OK!
TUN TUN
TUN TUN
TUN TUN
WHAT? THE TRAIN'S MOVING!
MENACED BY FRIEDA THE ENGINEERS START THE TRAIN DOWN THE TRACK.
AT LAST, WE'RE MOVING OUT OF THIS DAMN STATION!
STOP! STOP! ARE YOU CRAZY?
SNCF
WO TON
WO TON
WO TON
HEY! WE'RE MOVING!
IT CAN'T BE! THE DRIVERS HAVE GONE NUTS!
WO TON
WO TON
WO TON
DIN DON
ATTENTION! ATTENTION! WE WOULD LIKE TO INFORM PASSENGERS THAT WE ARE NOW LEAVING VARENNE STATION AT FULL SPEED! WE WISH YOU A PLEASANT JOURNEY ON THE "FRIEDA EXPRESS!"
WRUM
VOICE OF MISTRESS FRIEDA?
AS FOR YOU, NECRON, STOP THIS BULLSHIT AND JOIN ME IN THE DRIVER'S CAR.
HUH?

WAS VOICE OF MISTRESS FRIEDA... BUT WHERE IS MISTRESS?
PERHAPS MISTRESS INVISIBLE?
NECRON FEAR EVIL POWERS...
COURAGE, DUPONT! WE'RE APPROACHING THE ENGINE!
GO AND SEE WHAT'S HAPPENED TO THE TWO DRIVERS.
WELL, I DON'T KNOW IF THAT WOULD BE PRUDENT.
IT CRUSHED TRUDEAU'S HEAD LIKE A NUT! YOU SHOULD HAVE SEEN IT. ENORMOUS! A REAL MONSTER!
A MONSTER, HUH?
THEM CALL ME MONSTER?
NECRON NOT MONSTER!
NECRON CIVILIZED...
CRAK
AH!
...BUT NECRON ANGRY!
SKRUNK
RATATAT
SIGH!
NECRON! AT LAST!

WELL?
NECRON SORRY! PITY, MISTRESS, NOT PUNISH!
FOR ONCE YOU'VE DONE SOMETHING RIGHT. THOSE TWO WOULD HAVE SURPRISED ME!
WHO'S SHE TALKING TO?
AN ACCOMPLICE!
ME READY!
KEEP GUARD AND GIVE HELL TO ANYONE WHO COMES NEAR.
WHERE ARE WE EXACTLY?
NEAR LILLE, FIVE MINUTES FROM THE SCHEDULED STOP.
STEP ON IT!
GULP!
LILLE
WROOOAAAAMMM
HEY!
ASSHOLE!
TUDUM TUDUM TUDUM TUDUM
AM I WRONG, OR WAS THAT THE AMSTERDAM EXPRESS?
...SO EXPRESS IT DIDN'T STOP!
TUDUM TUDUM TUDUM TUDUM
WE'D BETTER NOTIFY THE BORDER! AT THAT SPEED, THEY'LL BE IN MOUSCRON IN A FLASH!
...AND STILL PACKED!
TUDUM

AT THE BELGIAN BORDER...
EXPRESS 613 FOR AMSTERDAM... OK. WE'LL WARN THE CONTROL CENTER.
SURE. WE'LL STOP IT. IF IT DOESN'T STOP AT THE BARRIER, WE'LL DIVERT THEM ONTO AN UNUSED TRACK. YOU CAN COUNT ON IT!
WHY ARE YOU SLOWING DOWN, DOLT?
IT'S AN OBLIGATORY STOP! WE'RE AT THE BORDER, CAN'T YOU SEE THE RED LIGHT?
I'M SICK OF RED LIGHTS, ACCELERATE!
THE EXPRESS CROSSES THE BORDER AT BREAKNECK SPEED.
613
SNCF
WRRROOOAAAMM
HERE WE ARE IN BELGIUM. BUT THESE TWO KNOW TOO MUCH!
TOO MANY PEOPLE HAVE ALREADY SEEN NECRON IN THE OPEN...

...BUT THERE WON'T BE ANYONE WHO CAN SQUEAL ON DOCTOR FRIEDA BOHER!
BANG
...GOOD JOB, TOO!
BANG
AH!
NECRON!
THROW THEM OUT!
NECRON OBEY MISTRESS!
SFRASC
PERFECT!... AND NOW TO ESCAPE!
LOOK, NECRON! I TURN THIS WHEEL AND THE TRAIN SLOWS DOWN.
OOH!
LOOK! NOW, WE'RE GOING AT WALKING PACE!
IT'S TRUE! WHAT'S GOING ON NOW?

DO YOU GET IT?
YES!
TUM TUM TUM TUM
NECRON TURN LIKE THIS...
OFF I GO!
TUM TUM TUM TUM
...AND THE TRAIN GO FAST! NECRON JUMP OUT!
WRROOAMM
RATAKRASH
RASH
KATASH
URG!
RASH
KATASH
KATAKRASH
GROWL!
KRASH
OH! NECRON BROKEN!
STUPID BEAST! IT'S YOUR FAULT! AND THE MONEY AND JEWELS THAT I ENTRUSTED TO YOU?
NECRON LOSE THEM!

BAH! NEVER MIND! I'LL MEND YOU. LUCKILY, IT'S NOTHING SERIOUS. FIRST, LET'S GET ON OUR WAY!
THE FOLLOWING NIGHT IN A FARMYARD BARN.
TRAIN DISASTER 136 VICTIMS BOTH DRIVERS SHOT IN THE HEAD.
PERFECT! WONDERFUL!
WE MADE A MESS OF THEM ALL RIGHT! HOW DO YOU FEEL NOW?
NECRON BETTER!
AND NOW YOU'RE AS GOOD AS NEW!
MISTRESS FORGIVE NECRON?
CLIK
NO! THIS LAST SET OF ESCAPADES IS ENOUGH TO DESERVE TEN YEARS OF ABSTINENCE!
BUT THE MASSACRE YOU ACCOMPLISHED ON THE TRAIN ENTERTAINED ME. YOU'VE EARNED A LITTLE TREAT BEFORE YOUR PENANCE...